Obsession

First Time, Rough Swingers, Kinky Family, Eroctica

Short Stories for Women Daddy

Lana Kendra

1

it wasn't bought for your personal use only, go back to your favorite ebook retailer and buy your copy. Thank you for acknowledging this author's efforts.

Table of Contents

Content Warning

Due to its sexual content, this book is only for those over the age of legal adulthood. There are some topics with a lot of foul language. All of the characters are at least eighteen years old.

Introduction

Are you in search of an exciting and thrilling book to read? Look no further than this extensive collection of Erotic Suspense book. I offer a wide range of genres, including Erotic Romantic Erotica, Fantasy, and Urban BDSM Fiction, to cater to even the most discerning reader. Whether you enjoy Anthologies, Westerns, or Paranormal Romance, I have something to suit your taste. My collection also includes Poetic Folklore, Interracial, Black & African American Literary Criticism, and Gothic Horror for those who crave a deeper and darker reading experience. If you're interested in Futuristic, LGBTQ+, Short Stories, or Lesbian literature, my diverse range of options will keep you captivated. Additionally, I offer Humorous, Victorian, New Adult, and College Women's Psychological Mysteries for those seeking a lighter but equally engaging read. Furthermore, My Fairy Tale Collections,

Transgender, Contemporary Western, Bisexual, and Poetry genres will transport you to different worlds and explore a variety of themes. For my Teen and Young Adult readers, I have a selection of European Geography, Cultures, eBooks, Loners, Outcasts, Mythology, Folk Tales, and much more. With such a wide array of options to choose from, you'll never run out of thrilling and enchanting stories to immerse yourself in.

It is important to emphasize that this content is exclusively intended for individuals who are 18 years of age or older.

Obsession

Fortunately, I arrived at the meeting just in time for the opening remarks despite being nearly late. The meeting had just been called to order by the woman at the front of the hall.

"First of all, before we begin our meeting, is there anyone that is here for their very first time?"

Despite my natural shyness, I had to speak. I reluctantly raised my hand, taking a moment to compose myself before raising it. I received a pat on the shoulder from a woman seated in the row behind me who complimented me on my bravery. Many more grinned and nodded in agreement.

"I am."

The woman smiled at me, making me feel comfortable.

"Welcome to our group! Would you care to come up to the

podium and introduce yourself, and perhaps share your story with us?"

"Alright, thank you, I will."

I moved to the front of the room, where I was given a glass of water, and I took a moment to look around at all the faces. After gathering my courage, I started talking.

"My name is Kathleen Connelly and I'm powerless over sex."

"Hello Kathleen!" the women crammed into the vast hall exclaimed collectively.

I cleared my throat, took a big gulp of water from my glass, and continued.

"I'm not exactly sure how to begin. Maybe I should start by saying that people would never suspect underneath my prim and proper middle class exterior I have an intense craving for large black cocks. I love everything about them from their taste to their texture to their musky smell. It might surprise you to know my husband is supportive of my obsession. While my marriage is perhaps somewhat unconventional before you judge me I'd like you to hear how our lifestyle evolved."

I glanced around the room to make sure no one was staring at me with disapproval, so I continued with my story.

"I think that our kids were the one who started it all. I adore them, but they have a lot of energy, and last year their behavior got to me. I was just tired and needed a vacation. I always thought that having kids would have been so much easier if I had started them earlier in life when I was younger and had more stamina.

Oh, I almost forgot to mention that they are twins. Having one girl go through puberty would be hard enough, but having two of them was a recipe for trouble. Anyway, my point is that the girl's boisterous behavior was making my husband and I desperate for some relief, so we decided to send them to Camp Cayuga, a well-known summer camp in the Poconos, even though the fees were higher than I would have preferred to pay because it had a long list of enjoyable activities for the kids to enjoy, making it easy to convince them to go. By the time school ended, I would have gladly paid twice what the camp requested because I felt it would have been money well spent.

Stanley and I went home after dropping the twins off at their camp, celebrated our newfound freedom with a bottle of champagne, told ourselves we had made the right choice, and then got down to a relaxing summer.

Every day during his lunch break, my husband calls me to catch up on the latest office gossip and discuss the goings-on in the neighborhood, but on this particular day, he seemed to be thinking about something else. Since I know that whenever he pauses in conversation, it usually means he is having trouble coming up with something to say, I finally told him to just stop circling the issue and say whatever it was he wanted to say.

"All right, Kathleen, I can't fool you," he said. I have to know about something that happened last night. I want you to be honest now. You did appreciate it, weren't you just putting it on?"

"Yes, Stanley, I did," I answered. "I wouldn't lie to you." The sex was fantastic!"

"Good," he remarked, appearing relieved. "Remember what we were discussing when you arrived?"

"Yes, honey," I said with a flush. "Of course I do."

Like most middle-aged couples with hyperactive kids, we had essentially lost our sexual life. Now that the girls were at camp, it came back to life almost immediately. We got some solitude for the first time in years, so we started experimenting to improve our love lives. Before we knew it, Stanley's closet was crammed with sexual films, and my night table drawer was overflowing with different sorts of vibrators. Stanley and I resembled two children let loose in a confectionery.

Stanley got a digital camera, and I bought myself a bunch of skimpy underwear to go along with our newfound freedom. In fact, he was able to persuade me to pose for him in my new underwear, which astonished me with how much it turned me on.

Stanley told me what was on his mind, and I was astonished. He had asked me directly if I would have sex with another man if given the chance to do so on a real basis.

Stanley was talking about our shared fantasy in which I saw myself having sex with a well-to-do black man while he looked on. After experimenting with the various adult video genres, we discovered that the ones regarding interracial cuckolding piqued our interest the most. Put simply, we became engrossed and quickly started acting out scenes from movies, imagining ourselves as the partners.

I was still a little awkward about our new fantasy existence, even though I was enjoying it a lot, and it sounded tacky and cheap to hear Stanley discuss it over the phone. It appeared as though he had violated a tacit understanding that our fantasies would stay in the bedroom. I know it seems ridiculous, but I thought that talking about them openly would somehow make them come to life. He seemed a little uncomfortable because it was the first time he had ever brought up the topic outside of when we were making love. I reluctantly consented, figuring he was just repeating his fantasy from the night before.

"I...I think I could," I nervously replied. "I mean if you were really, really sure that's what you wanted. But it would have to be with someone I liked. I couldn't just do it with anyone. And besides," I replied with a sense of relief, "we don't know any black people."

"Oh yes we do." Stanley said to me. "I have some interesting news for you. You know Robert Jeffries, the nice young black fellow that used to work with me, the one that we've been fantasizing about?"

I said, "What about him, Stanley?"

"Well, prepare yourself for this," Stanley replied. "Robert's going to be my new assistant."

My heart started racing in my chest. The mere mention of Robert's name made me want to cry. My spouse was using the fact that I had a crush on Robert to make me feel agitated. We had been viewing a film of a much younger Black man fucking a White wife, since that's exactly what they were doing. I was so attracted to it that, in a moment of weakness, I admitted to Stanley that I could see myself having sex with Robert. It had looked harmless enough, since he was no longer employed at Stanley's office.

I chastised him, praying in my heart that he was telling the truth, "Don't tease me like that!" Robert was the one who could really get my creative juices going. Robert and I had first connected during a summer picnic organized by Stanley's company around three years prior, and since then, we had been utilizing him frequently in our dreams.

Despite being fifteen years younger than me, Robert was the first African American I had really met and I fell in love with him the instant I lay eyes on him. He was the most gorgeous young man I had ever seen. He was very tall, had skin the color of coffee, a shaved head, and a smile that would melt butter.

We had a few "brothers" in college, but they kept to themselves pretty well; the only information I had about them came from my good friend Ellen Barclay, who had fallen in love with Tyrell Cleaver, the school football team's handsome black quarterback, despite all the jeers she had received from her peers.

As the most sexually active of all my girlfriends—and trust me, she'd seen a lot of them—Elena told me in one of our more open discussions that Tyrell had the biggest blackest cock she'd ever seen.

I suppose you could say that Ellen had planted the seed, since she took great pleasure in telling us girls about her various adventures, which gave us all a very thorough, if not graphic, sexual education; she would positively glow when she told us how well-endowed Tyrell was, and often trotted out that old cliché, once you go black you never go back. But because of her experience and forthrightness, you sensed that she was telling the truth; her detailed account of what it was like to suck cum out of a big black cock particularly fascinated me.

Ever since my fascination with black men began in college, I suppose my attraction to Robert was inevitable. I'd only met him once at the picnic and ran into him a couple of times at Stanley's office, but every time I saw him, I couldn't help but stare at the noticeable bulge in his pants. I tried not to show my interest, but I think he sensed it because he began making out with me behind Stanley's back, and before I knew it, I was falling hard for him. Fortunately, the firm moved Robert to their Topeka branch before I could ruin myself.

I have been told by many, including my husband, that I have a nice figure and that my long brown hair is very attractive, so I guess self-esteem was never a problem for me. Nevertheless, I must admit that although, or rather should I say because Robert was so much younger, his discreet flirting had been very flattering, if not downright exciting.

It's real, honey. Stanley stated in a serious tone, "He truly is going to be my assistant. I believed he was gone for good when he was transferred, but our branch in Kansas closed, so he was brought back. It was quite the coincidence that he arrived, considering everything we've been discussing lately. We thought it would be a great chance to realize our fantasy. I've invited him to supper tonight since he'll be working for me once more. His level of curiosity has increased, so we might have an overnight visitor."

"Do you mean he's lost interest in you?"I hope Stanley hasn't told Robert about our fantasies," I replied, blushing and feeling sick to my stomach.

Stanley said, "Of course not, but I did fan the fires a little." There was a little silence before he continued, "We were playing around on my computer today, and I showed him your images. He adored them all, but he especially paid attention when I showed him the ones where you were holding your black baby dolls."

The majority of the photos were pretty innocent, but the ones he was referring to were positively obscene; the sheer sheerness of the wispy little garment made it obvious that my nipples were excited, and the fact that I had no underwear on made it abundantly clear that my pussy was extremely wet and hairy. The pictures were meant to be exclusive to Stanley.

"Oh, Stanley, you bastard," I sobbed. "Please keep those to yourself. How in the world will he perceive me? I feel like an extremely foolish old slut."

I had been unconsciously masturbating myself as my husband talked about bringing Robert home, and despite what I was saying, the thought of Robert staring at my nudity was getting me pretty aroused, and as I spoke to Stanley, my hand had stolen up my skirt and under the leg band of my panties. Feeling how wet I was getting, I realized I could hardly wait to carry on with our interrupted flirtation, and I was already thinking about what I should wear that night.

Stanley tried to calm my worries by saying, "You don't

have to worry about Robert thinking that of you Kathleen. After all, he does work at our photographic studio. He told me I was a very lucky man and that you had a wonderful body. He even declared that you were much more attractive than any of the younger models we ever utilize for our photo shoots.

Honestly? Did he truly say that?My clitoris throbbed with lust, aching for the relief that could only come from a good stiff cock, as I gasped and felt a warm glow spreading up from between my legs and washing over my tummy. By now, my nipples had fully erect and were pushing out the front of my light cotton shift. I wondered what might happen that night if I really let myself go.

"Yes, honey," my spouse continued. "He stated you were even more beautiful than he had imagined. I saw the young man had a lot going on while he was gazing at your photos. To be honest, I wouldn't be shocked if he overreacts and starts seeing you tonight. Well, it wouldn't bother me if he did. How far you want to go is entirely up to you."

Would that really be alright with you, Stanley?"Are you positive you wouldn't get upset with me or jealous?" I questioned. Like you, I find the concept thrilling, but I wouldn't want to take any actions that would endanger our marriage. You understand that nothing will ever be the same again if I do fuck Robert. I wish for you to be regret-free.

Stanley reassured me, "I won't, honey. The idea of you fucking Robert in our bed erases any jealousy I might have." My own cock is dripping when I imagine that enormous black whopper of his into your tight tiny pussy. I think my erection would allow me to pole jump."

"Stanley," I said, "I know it's inappropriate, but the thought is really gratifying." Is Robert really that huge of a cock? How are you aware of that?"

Stanley laughed and said, "I saw him coming out of the

shower room after the company's golf tournament." His eyes widened.

"I promise, his balls dangle like a pair of grapefruits, and his cock appears to be at least a foot long! They must contain a large number of infants. It's fortunate that you had your tubes closed, as it would be quite challenging to justify a small black brother to the twins. Nevertheless, I apologize, but I have to leave; I was just summoned for a meeting. By seven o'clock tonight, we need to be at the house."

I begged, "Oh god Stanley, please help me a little. What shall I serve? For me to wear, what do you want? All of this is totally unforeseen."

Stanley was absolutely useless.

"I really do have to go now, but I'll leave those things up to you, baby. I'm sure whatever you do will be fine." "We'll see you later tonight," he promised. Sweetheart, bye."

I was in a genuine tizzy after Stanley had phoned, dropped his bombshell, then hung up so abruptly. I wanted to take things one step at a time and make sure tonight was flawless, so I purposefully got myself a lovely cup of tea to settle down my racing mind.

I could use the pool to my advantage if all went well tonight, but fortunately our pool had been serviced the week before and the gardener had just mowed the yard, so I didn't have to worry about anything outside.

I had planned to buy three of the best steaks I could find from the neighborhood butcher; I had chosen steak specifically because I knew Robert loved barbecue, and I wanted to make him feel right at home. After the butcher had trimmed and wrapped the filets, I went to the liquor store and asked the clerk to help me choose three nice bottles of Napa Valley Cabernet Sauvignon. Now that I had taken care of the two most important ingredients, I drove to the grocers to find some fresh vegetables and something rich and appropriate for dessert.

Back at home, I made most of the dinner fixings ahead of time so that it would all look as easy as possible, then I sat down to calm myself with a glass of sherry; looking at my watch, I realized I had four more torturous hours of waiting for Stanley to bring Robert home.

In an attempt to decompress, I took a nice hot bubble bath at six o'clock. After soaking for twenty minutes, I toweled off, sprayed some Estee Lauder Spellbound on my most private areas, put on my lacey white Décolleté bra and some brand-new white silk panties, and arranged some of my sexier casual outfits on the bed.

When I was fully dressed, I painted my lips a deep rich burgundy, put on my cultured pearl necklace, and strapped on my new four-inch white patent pumps. I looked myself over in my full-length mirror and grinned at what I saw. I can definitely understand why we older women are called cougars. I finally settled on my favorite skintight white Capri pants and a turquoise v-neck angora sweater.

Still feeling butterflies in my stomach, I poured myself another large glass of sherry. As I was sipping my drink, I heard Stanley's car pull into the driveway, and my heart leaped up and I ran to the front door, feeling like a little girl on her first date. I opened the door with great anticipation, remembering every word we said that evening.

You're in this place, Mrs. Connelly!Robert said in a deep, very silky voice.

Stanley was close behind him, looking very happy with himself, and he towered over me like a black Adonis, flashing a mouthful of sparkling pearly teeth and holding out a lovely bouquet of huge pink roses tangled with white baby's breath.

"Ah, Robert, they... They're stunning!I gave him a quick

peck on the cheek and noticed that he had been drinking, which I took as a positive indication since it indicated that he was probably just as apprehensive as I was. "I mumbled, grinning awkwardly.

"Thank you so much, I'll just go put these in some water."

He responded, "They're not as beautiful as you are, Mrs. Connelly," and Stanley led him into the living room. "No offense Mr. Connelly, but I'm not going to let your wife get away with just a quick peck on the cheek," he stated in a bold moment. I believe I should at the very least receive a hearty kiss!"

My finest crystal vase was located, and as I filled it with water, I marveled at how effortlessly everything was falling into place; maybe, I thought to myself, Robert's big black cock would too, before the night was over. I carried the full vase of flowers back to the living room and placed it on the coffee table, adding to the raw sensuality that filled the space.

"Robert, where did you find such beautiful flowers?Feeling quite honored, I questioned, "I don't think I've ever seen roses that huge before. They're just incredible!"

"They really are large, don't they? I had planned to give you some baby roses, but after seeing them, I decided against it. I assumed you were the kind of woman who enjoys larger-than-life objects."

Robert wrapped his arms around me to give me a hug and murmured in my ear; it felt so intimate to have him so close that I would have quickly changed out of my underwear if he had asked. He gave me a knowing smile, and I'm sure I blushed six colors of crimson.

"Miss. I apologize, Connelly, but I just can't stop thinking about you during my entire trip to Kansas!"

That's when he picked me up as easily as a sack of feathers

and planted a kiss on me so passionately that it sent shivers down my spine. My arms instinctively wrapped around his neck and I clung to him as he spun me around the room, his full, soft lips covering mine as I tried, with what little willpower I had left, to keep my tongue from sliding between his teeth and into his warm, wet mouth.

To my immense dismay, Robert tenderly lowered me to the ground after what felt like an endless period of happiness. I noticed passion mixed with angst on Stanley's face as I turned to see how he was handling everything. I attempted to reassure him with a grin. We stood there in awkward quiet, the three of us. Since none of us knew exactly how to proceed, we were all novices at this.

Stanley broke the peace with a faint cough. "May I get drinks for everyone?" he inquired.

"Dear, that would be amazing," I answered. "I've just been having a glass of sherry." I turned to face Robert. "How about you Robert, what would you like?"

Robert said, "Sherry sounds good to me," and I felt like wringing out my dainties.

After Stanley delivered our drinks, we spent the next hour talking about Robert's work back in Kansas and our kids' summer camp. Stanley then asked if Robert had ever been with any ladies, changing the topic.

"Well, my young marriage proved to be an absolute nightmare. I believe that for some of us males, it's probably best to stay single." He gave me a friendly wink. "I'm good at making babies Mrs. Connelly, but I'm terrible at raising them."

"I meant while you were in Topeka." Stanley added his voice, seeming rather irritated.

"No, I'm afraid I've been far too busy for that Mr. Connelly, although last winter I certainly could have used a nice lady to keep me warm," he replied with a grin. "Southern

California is nothing like Kansas. There, the winters can be quite chilly. Say, is it only me, or is this place getting pretty hot?

"It's not just you Robert, it is very hot in here." And I agreed. "You're welcome to bring our beverages outside to the patio. Before supper, we could even have a quick swim in the pool. It sounds like a pleasant way to unwind."

"That sounds like a wonderful idea, I'd love to take you up on it but I'm afraid I don't have any swimming trunks."

"That is not an issue. Stanley has an additional pair available for your use.

"Thank you, Mrs. Connelly. If it's okay with you, I'd prefer to wait until after dinner. It would be awkward to have my stomach rumbling the entire time we were in the pool, and I'm hungry enough to eat a horse."

Of course. I apologize; I was virtually blind to the fact that we had dinner. Stanley, lead Robert outside to the patio while I start preparing the steaks. We can eat outside by the swimming area.

I started by setting out some of my handmade Dungeness crab cakes with poblano chile sauce and opened the first bottle of cabernet sauvignon while the steaks were grilling. The wine and crab cakes disappeared quickly, so I served a straightforward salad of tomatoes and onions with provolone cheese and excused myself to fetch the steaks. I served them with baked potatoes and cheddar, a big dollop of sour cream flavored with chives, and some fresh asparagus wrapped in puff pastry on my finest Noritake china. I proudly brought them out to the table, grinning.

"Oh Mrs. Connelly, what an incredible woman you are!" When I put Robert's food in front of him, he cried out. "This appears fantastic. It's unbelievable that you went to such lengths."

"Why, Robert, it wasn't at all difficult. I simply combined

what I had. Regretfully, it was my best option given the short notice."

As he sliced into his rare filet mignon, I silently prayed and then exhaled a breath of relief. Just as he'd requested, it was medium rare.

"I hope you understand how fortunate you are, Mr. Connelly. This steak is flawless. Your spouse is not only stunning, but she also makes delicious food."

All of his compliments made me flush. I could feel the wine starting to take effect and get really horny. I returned the ball to Robert's domain.

"Young fellow, please stop doing that right away or I might lose myself in you! Did I really just say that? Oh my god. I have to be careful how much I drink tonight—you never know what can occur!"

Taking my hint, Robert grinned, retrieved Stanley's wine bottle, and filled my glass again. Nothing could be confused about his intentions.

Robert and I laced our discussion during our meal with suggestive remarks about sex. Although neither of us was brave enough to discuss the direction the evening may take directly, there was an almost tangible sexual tension in the air. Stanley, poor old man, did his best to act casually and kept the wine coming. I could have fooled everyone, even a blind man, with the meaningful glances Robert and I were sharing that night that I was going to get screwed.

We had my blackberry apple crumble with crème fraiche and freshly brewed espresso to cap off our dinner. I got my husband to bring Robert inside so he could put on his beach suit while I got dressed in my bikini. I believe Stanley had decided it was time to abandon his idea since he was losing courage.

"Honey, that's been on my mind. I had a rather tiny bathing suit. I'm definitely lot bigger than I am in that region, yet it barely fits me." He became very red upon admitting it.

"Why Stanley, what are you suggesting?"

"Well, I really doubt if Robert would be able to get it on, and even if he could it wouldn't be very comfortable, so perhaps we should forget about the swimming tonight."

"Nonsense!" said I. Here, we're all close friends, and Robert is starting to feel like a member of the group. When we're alone, we hardly never wear bathing suits."

Feeling rather red from all the wine we'd consumed, I turned to face Robert. The time had come. We had started mating in earnest.

"I'm certainly game if you are." I spoke, reinforcing my blatant double entendre by staring into his eyes. Robert looked back at me.

I said, stating the obvious, "We don't do this when the girls are at home," nearly stumbling as I hopped around, trying to quickly take off my Capri pants.

"No, of course you don't," he shot back, keeping his gaze fixed on my eyes while removing his shirt to display his well-defined chest. With caution, he hung his shirt on the back of his chair and started unbuckling his pants. With his eyes fixed on mine, he gradually lowered his pants. I shrugged out of my sweatshirt and undid my bra in accordance.

I looked over at Stanley, who was watching the two of us while slyly stroking his cock through his pants. He dropped his eyes in embarrassment when he saw my expression. With a foolish smile on my face, I turned to face Robert again and was excited to see his silk boxers stretched way out in front.

"God Mrs. Connelly, you're getting me so fucking horny!" Robert murmured, folding his pants and glancing all over me. His cock shot up and smacked his belly button with an audible slap. I started drooling as soon as he took off his shorts because I remembered my former friend Ellen telling me how much she liked to suck off attractive black men.

My clitoris pounded as I took off my little underwear and gave it to Stanley, making sure he took part in my offering to Robert. I took charge of the matter because he appeared uncertain and reluctant to move forward.

Stanley, please remove your clothing as well. You intended for this to occur. Don't start to feel uneasy just yet. Robert is going to fuck me. Whether you want to participate in it or not is up to you, but it will undoubtedly occur."

Robert responded, "Yeah, come on Mr. Connelly," with a tone that surprised everyone. "Aim to be at ease with it. Go fetch your camera and don't give up on us."

Robert scooped me up and carried me into the living room, where he lay me down on the chaise lounge, all pretense gone.

Stanley, poor guy, trailed behind. He struggled to make a

decision. He appeared to be scared of missing anything, even if he wished to follow Robert's advice. I reclined on the couch and supported my torso with my elbows.

I responded, "It's okay, honey," in a deep, passionate voice that was beginning to shatter. "Go get your little camera, we won't begin without you."

Though Robert and I had the best of intentions, things had already begun to move quickly as Stanley got back. It had proven to be far too tempting for me to be so close to Robert's pulsating manhood. I prostrated myself before him, suckling on his fully developed black cock while he caressed my swelling teats. The abrupt camera light brought back memories of my assurance to Stanley that we would wait for him.

Oddly enough, I laughed so hard I nearly choked on Robert's popcorn as I recalled a sermon I'd heard about how the path to hell is paved with good intentions. I may be heading to hell in a handcart, but it will definitely be worth it, I reasoned.

"Oh god Mrs. Connelly, I've got to stop or I'm liable to explode!" Reluctantly pulling himself out from between my jism-coated lips, Robert gasped. His young, strong, black cock was still attached to my tongue by the long string of come that swayed in the air between us as I gazed in fascination. I couldn't decide whether to let him fuck me or put him back in my mouth. Stanley decided what was best for us.

He snapped his camera at our vile behavior, choking, "Fuck her son, go on.... give the dirty whore what she needs!"

Robert's lustful eyes went glassy as his masculine authority seized center stage.

"Mr. Connelly, could you please help me out? Would you kindly lie down on the lounge on your back? While I'm fucking your wife for you, you ought to have a nice view."

As Robert advised, Stephen took a seat on the lounge and waited.

Alright! I want you to turn around and straddle him now, Mrs. Connelly."

Robert pushed me forward on my elbows after I'd straddled my husband, putting my pussy squarely over Stanley's face and putting me in the dog position. Robert approached me from behind and placed his penis at the entrance of my cunt. Stanley's wife's pouting pussy was going to swallow a much larger and more robust black man's cock, and I watched his cock rise in the air and heard him whimper.

"Mr. Connelly, do you really want me to fuck your wife?" Robert enquired. "Aren't you afraid that once she gets a taste for it she's going to want it more and more?"

"Fuck me Robert!" Please don't make fun of me! Tell him

to fuck me, Stanley, please! Oh my gosh!"

I was pimping out to his young black companion, and Stanley enjoyed the process of holding my swollen pussylips apart. I pressed my soft round buttocks back into Robert as he nuzzled his head of cock into my hole. I could feel my body becoming more damp to fit his enormous girth.

"Fuck the dirty bitch!" Stanley sniffed. He was no longer a willing participant in his own cuckolding because his lust had overcome his uncertainty.

Robert followed my smell and, with his velvety black battering ram, invaded the deep corners of my womb by clutching my waist. His cock exploded of its own accord, its hefty load of thick, gooey cream shooting through the air and landing on my nose and glasses. Stanley's vantage point was too much for him. Having my husband's semen drip off my chin while his young protégé hammered on my cunt made me feel like such a slut. Robert suddenly roared loudly and emptied his balls into me.

Ladies, allow me to explain. I was completely pushed over the brink by all that newly made, scalding hot cum being blasted inside of me. I had the longest, loudest, strongest orgasm I had ever had, and I started to thrash and moan like a wounded animal. I used to scream so much that Stanley had to cover my lips with his palm to keep the neighbors from hearing me.

When I eventually emerged from wherever I had been, I turned to face my husband. Stanley was growing tired and his hangover from all the wine we'd drunk had taken its toll. Amazingly, my young black beau was still erect even though he was lying on his back.

Who, after all, could decline such an invitation? Stanley was sleeping as I moved down onto his huge black cock and we resumed our rutting. Robert took a little longer to arrive this time, but I can say without a doubt that it was well worth the wait. This attempt was even better than the previous one, suggesting that the original attempt was really an experiment. When we were all done, I was in complete amazement. I was taken with such deft intensity that only a genuinely well-fucked woman could possibly comprehend.

We then swam in the pool and had some more wine. Robert scooped me up in his arms, brought me back to our bedroom, and we left again, so I guess the pool wasn't enough to quell his passion. By morning, I was practically pleading with Robert to stop because I was so hurt. Stanley, poor Stanley, slept through the whole night and never got to witness me being taken by Robert in our marriage bed.

I believe my spouse may have ended up with far more than he had anticipated, even though his original request had been for sloppy seconds. The following day, Stanley watched as I fucked four more of Robert's "brothers," both singly and in different combinations.

Word has now spread that I find it impossible to turn down a large, black cock. I am virtually always entertaining well-groomed black males because it has gotten out of control. I'm going to permanently send the twins to boarding school after their summer camp experience so they won't have to witness their mother's transformation into a slutty person. There you have it, then. That is my narrative. Thank you so much for listening, everyone."

After a protracted awkward pause, a woman from the back row got up and began to clap, and the entire room erupted in thunderous applause. After the applause subsided and every woman had taken a seat, the chairperson finally spoke up.

"Yes...ah...well thank you for sharing Kathleen...Kathleen, there is help for you if you really want to stop doing what you're doing.."

I'm sorry, but I don't want to stop. Thank you. I'm not here for that reason. It appears that I've gone full circle and am now confronting my initial issue once more. You know, I need a break. I'm tired from dealing with so many attractive young black males. I was hoping someone would be interested in getting rid of a couple of these.

In their rush to be selected, the women pushed each other aside and pressed forward.

One of them exclaimed, "I'll help you Kathleen!"

Another woman exclaimed, "Me too!"

One more begged, "No let me!" while another said, "And me!"

Another yelled, "I'll be happy to help you fuck them!"

This was going to be much simpler than I had anticipated. There sure looked to be plenty of assistance available to solve my problem.

Acknowledgments

The Glory of this book's success goes to God Almighty and my beautiful Family, Fans, Readers & well-wishers, Customers, and Friends for their endless support and encouragement.

About The Author

I've spent nearly a decade penning romantic novels. As a passionate writer of erotica, I craft dark, romantic erotica. Anime Naked Truth Se of Sacred Sexuality: Forbidden Seducing Short Stories of an Erotica Nude Sexy Girl Poster. Alongside Erotic Mystery Fiction, Victorian Erotica Sex, Black & African American Erotica, Euthanasia, Daddy Teaching, Forced Domination, Alpha Monster Cuckold, and BDSM for Adults, there's an Erotic Fiction in Kinky Family. I write dark, sensual romance because I adore the power of darkness and everything that it entails. Romance novels have always been my favorite kind of books, and now I'm writing them. The idea that you will like reading and enjoying my fiction as much as I enjoy pushing the frontiers of sexual pleasure in my writing thrills me more than anything else.